E
EMB

Emberley, Ed.
Thanks, Mom

E
EMB

Emberley, Ed.
Thanks, Mom

8-17-04

THANKS, MOM

by Ed Emberley

LITTLE, BROWN AND COMPANY   BOSTON   NEW YORK   LONDON

STARRING

OTTO the Outrageous!

KOKO AND KIKO the Courageous!

FIDO *the Fabulous!*

MUMBO *the Marvelous!*

GATO *the Glorious!*

Oh, Kiko, see the cheese?

Run, Kiko, run!
But don't drop that delicious cheese!

Oh, Kiko, see Gato?

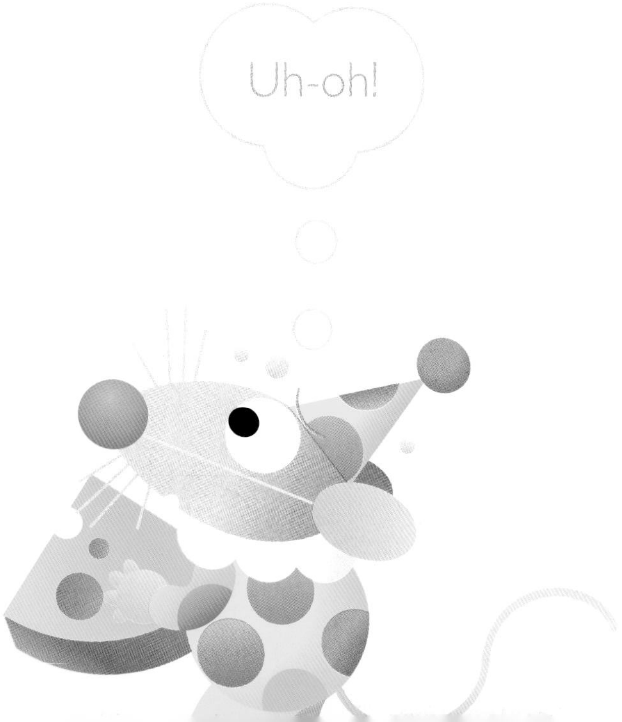
Uh-oh!

See Gato run?

Run, Kiko, run!
But don't drop that delicious cheese!

Oh, Gato, see Fido?

See Fido run?

Run, Gato, run!

Run, Kiko, run!
But don't drop that delicious cheese!

Oh, Fido, see Otto?

See Otto run?

Run, Fido, run!   Run, Gato, run!   Run, Kiko, run!
But don't drop that delicious cheese!

Oh, Otto, see Mumbo?

See Mumbo run?

Run, Otto, run!   Run, Fido, run!   Run, Gato, run!   Run, Kiko, run!
But don't drop that delicious cheese!

Oh, Mumbo, see Koko?

See Koko run?

Run, Mumbo, run!   Run, Otto, run!   Run, Fido, run!   Run, Gato, run!

Run, Kiko, run! Run all the way home!

But don't drop that delicious cheese!

First Edition

ISBN 0-316-24022-2

LCCN 2001650715

10 9 8 7 6 5 4 3 2 1

TWP

Printed in Singapore